Bedside Stories

HOTELES

Bedside Stories

5

Ignacio Ferrando

Dionisio Martínez

Patricia Suárez

Eloy Serrano Barroso

Published by ©NH Hoteles

Director of the collection: José Luis Martín Nogales

Cover design: NH Hoteles Marketing Department

Collection design and mock-up: José Luis Martín Nogales

Printed by Castuera

Translated by Bianca Southwood

Legal Deposit: NA 1499/2005

On the 7 March 2005, a jury made up of Juan Luis Cebrián, Carmen Posadas, José Romera Castillo, Javier Tomeo and José Luis Martín Nogales awarded the following NH Mario Vargas Llosa Prizes for Short Stories:

Friends and Ghosts, by Mercedes Abad

Tales of Love and the North, by César Gavela

Babel, by Ignacio Ferrando

The finalists were:
Do Not Send Flowers to Your Mother, by Dionisio Martínez
The I Ching and the Papers Man, by Guillermo Martínez
Today You Won't Believe Me Either, Laura, by Manuel Francisco Rodríguez
Nativity Scenes, by Eloy Serrano
Chicken Paprika, by Patricia Suárez

CONTENTS

Ignacio Ferrando

Babel

*I*gnacio Ferrando was born in Trubia (Asturias) in 1972. He works as a quantity surveyor. He has written many short stories, some of which have been published in magazines and cultural supplements and others which have been included in recent collective anthologies. Quite a few are yet to be published. His first collection of short stories, <u>Historias de la mediocridad</u> (Stories of Mediocrity), was published in 2003.

<u>Babel</u>, which won him the NH Mario Vargas Llosa Prize, is the story about an important lesson: accepting that making futile endeavours will always lead to failure.

Babel

My father used to say that condoning one act of injustice can only lead to every other act of injustice. He was right. When it all began, Clara and I were just two youngsters living in that indulgent reality we call childhood. I remember how she used to play near the fountain, running around the fruit stalls, getting her knees all grazed up and jumping in and out of a skipping rope along with the other girls. We boys would spend our time dashing down the same narrow, bustling streets or chasing the cats which lived on the roofs. The day that Adolphe Thoreau, the new dean, came into town preceded by a whole retinue of theologians and dogmatists, we were the first too see him amidst the impermeable silence. Thoreau was seated in a black carriage pulled by two horses with red ribbons. Through the window, I was able to catch a glimpse of his distinguished Florentine bearing and the dark look of scorn with which he was contemplating the stir caused by his arrival. I remember that his carriage stopped in the middle of the commotion and the herald, a small, meek little man, read the edict aloud. The ring of his refined voice reached us over the racket made by the merchants and the boiling cauldrons. "It is the endeavour of the monsignor," he said, raising his voice, "to build a tower three thousand feet in height over the existing vault in Wescen Abbey for the praise and glory of the Lord. The construction work is to commence immediately…" He said other things too but the bit about building a tower over the abbey was left stamped on my mind, like an imperial mark in the jumbled amalgam of my memories.

Because we are nothing but memories. The present expires and leaves a wake of remembrances. Clara once told me that her memories were all selective and self-interested. "I suppose we only remember what helps us survive and forget the rest," she said.

Forty-two years later, from where I am perched up here on this brass pinnacle, I can still hear the echo of her words and I deplore the fact that, as my father would have said, I have become the victim of a string of injustices. Swallows are seldom mistaken in their predictions. It is going to rain. It is going to pour down tonight, with a northerly wind. The tower will be at risk. From up here, now that the job is completed, everything has taken on the same relativity as insignificant objects. People are no more perceptible than ants and Wescen is but a small cluster of clayey roofs that I could pick up with one hand and put down somewhere else. The river

Spree, now full after the low water, cuts through the meadow, blue and sparkling, and the paths and tracks twist and wind like ochre scars all the way to the horizon. Clara is smiling at me and the wind, blowing her dress and her long, silvery hair in the same direction, brings a strong waft of lavender. We barely fit on the same wooden platform, hanging in what seems like mid-air. There are no rails, no handles, no ropes to hang on to. We look into the distance like birds with the conscience of men, like dethroned demigods. The wooden boards tremble and crack like the teeth of a dying man. The struts have become twisted and the weak, zigzagging wooden structures, hammered in at impossible angles, threaten to topple and fall. The afternoon breeze rocks us as if we were an inverted pendulum. Clara and I kiss each other once again, at a strange angle, aware at last of the pendular nature of the Universe.

The height muffles any sound and turns it

into a kind of blur in the distance. We can only hear the sharp lashings of the wind and the restless sleep of the stonemasons who have collapsed into a slumber a few storeys down, their dreams spilling over like waterfalls into the void. Today is Monday. The Mondays of our childhood, at this same time, the second-hand dealers would gather up their pots and pans and hang them on the sides of their wagons. As they set off, they made a metallic, distant sound. If you closed your eyes you could imagine being on a battlefield and that around you, swords were clashing ferociously. My father would often take me with him to the market. He taught me how to buy the best steel nails, the straightest, the sharpest. He would put them on a piece of timber and knock them all the way in with just one blow. He also told me that the best woods were the ones with a straight grain, neither too old nor too green. "Elm," he would say, "elm and macerated oak are the best woods." He told me, as he held those orangey stones up against the light, what tone to look for in resins... And I feel the faint nostalgia of childhood and those years before Thoreau came to Wescen with the preposterous idea of building his tower.

My father had been the foreman of the construction work on the abbey. Before Thoreau appeared, he had been in charge of minor issues such as renovating the plaster on the façade, shoring up the vault before doing repair works on the guttering or installing his famous system of synchronous pulleys that in his day, allowed the bells to be struck in unison, thus creating a polyphony which can still be heard from miles away. In Wescen he was regarded as an upright, sensible man. Yet he had one great defect. Anyone who knew him will agree with me: he liked gold with the same foolish pleasure as a miser. He did not spend it, but rather amassed it like a fig tree accumulates its withered, milky resin, letting it dry uselessly on the bark of its tree. As far as I can remember, at home, in the home of my childhood that is, we never went hungry, but when Thoreau summoned him and asked him to build his tower, the gold proved too irresistible. My father's mistake was to confuse Thoreau's deliria with the dreams of a madman. It would seem, according to what my father told us, that he had had a dream in which God had spoken to him, prophesying that he would build the highest tower on the face of the Earth, a sort of vengeance of Babel, a reconstruction of ignominy. Thoreau liked to speak about the tower. He had seen it in dreams and talked of it as if it existed not very far away, a stylish construction with its copper-coloured outside and its svelte glass spire. "Through the immense leaded stained glass windows," he said, "the zenithal morning light will colour the walls with iridescent splendour and shades of salmon-pink, scaring off the shadows which creep into the chapels." The dean dreamed day and night but he was not insane. Sometimes he was seen meditating in the courtyard, watching from where he stood, pointing at the weather vane or the scaffolding we were working on. Suddenly, as if waking from a dream and seizing some idea in mid-air, he would start doodling in the pipe clay with a stick.

When my father saw the dean's project (the drawing of a huge spire three thousand feet high breaking through the blue outline of the clouds and soaring up to infinity) he threw up his hands in horror.

"The abbey was built on a wasteland," he replied. "Half of the buttresses were destroyed in the last lot of floods. It would not even be able to support a tenth of the weight of that spire. In any case, it would take decades..."

But Thoreau just ignored him. He ignored him then and he ignored him consistently thereafter. If God spoke to him, then that surely would outweigh any arithmetic reasoning and geometrical accuracy. He would evade the issue by saying things like "the Lord will provide," and "we must have faith in His intentions". With an associate like that, who was my father to quibble? I still cannot understand how he managed to persuade my father to start building. I imagine that even my father must have begun to believe in the divine legitimacy of the project.

"We will reinforce such-and-such flying buttress," he would say, pointing at the plan, observing Thoreau out of the corner of his eye. "We will shore it up with blocks of granite at the keystone and..."

And thus we began building the tower. Stonemasons from the surrounding towns were called in along with blacksmiths from the Alba guild and carpenters from the Angosta forest. One of them was Clara's father, although he had been living in Wescen for years. He was a widower, a hunchback with bristly eyebrows and a wicked look in his eyes, a man who seemed to have been swept along by the wind of necessity. Clara, on the other hand, was a girl with a shrewd, restless look about her. She spent most of her time watching her father hammering studs into planks of wood and climbing onto walkways. She would pass him his burin and his pliers and in summer, when it was hot, she would make sure the old man had enough wine to wet his whistle. One afternoon when we were all working on the tower, Thoreau sent the herald with a new message. "The building work," he read out, "is like priestly celibacy and must be carried out as an absolute and intimate act of devotion. As of today," the herald paused for a moment before continuing, "it is the wish and order of His Holiness that nobody, under any circumstances, shall leave the tower until the work is completed." And once again, the Lord was the excuse that would seal our sentence. With the authorization of the devil himself, may the Lord forgive me, the abbot locked the belfry doors, promising us eternal salvation and inconceivable fortunes once the project had finished. The deceit seeped through each of the syllables of his words, shaped by his doctrinaire lips.

A few months later we had set up the pulleys and several raising systems. My father always admired the Romans' pragmatism and considered them the fathers of modern construction.

"Not only did they use animals, they also relied on the strength nature has to offer," he would say to me.

For that reason, because of the Romans, he designed an oak tank to collect rainwater. When the pulleys were being set up, he hung wineskins off the ends that filled with the water from the tank. This way, using the wineskins as counterweights, the ashlars could be hauled up slowly with a regular movement under the supervision of the foremen and with minimum effort from the workers. The stones themselves, huge slabs of granite that had been torn out of the mountain, were loaded onto wooden rollers and then moved to their definitive position. For three or four years, the pulleys were constantly going up and down the hollow spire of the church and the stonemasons, from where they were working in the middle of the nave, never ceased chinking away at the stone with their chisels. From above, my father made sure that each piece coincided and fitted in perfectly according to Thoreau's plans.

Clara spent the day rushing around; following her father, running ahead of him and helping him carry buckets. Her father would tell her to calm down and go and sit in a corner quietly where she would not get hurt. We raised the first course. I remember that the circle was thirty metres in diameter. We had put some planks of wood over the shaft and my father was standing in the centre of one of them with a plan in his hand and a kind of huge compass, measuring the curve of what was to become the base of the tower.

"In architecture," he said, "the circle represents an impossible measurement. The circle is a longing for perfection in geometry. That is why, unlike other shapes, it requires greater precision, greater effort..."

And he would go over every possible radius, never tiring. And for the first two years, course upon course grew from the dome of the abbey.

The day that Clara became an orphan there was a storm. Tiny drops of rain fell upon the base of the cathedral, sliding down the lead fillings. The walkways were simply planks of wood a few inches thick that sagged under the weight of the stonemasons. The fact is that Clara's father could hardly see and the humidity had undermined his joints. He did not even flinch when, in the middle of a walkway, a stone hanging from the temporary tympanum hit him straight in the chest, throwing him a good distance in a parabolic swing with a look of fear on his face and the palms of his hands wide open, as if he had wanted to grab hold of the air.

Yes, tiny drops of rain fell upon the base of the cathedral. It is an image which appears repeatedly in Clara's nightmares. The drops become puddles, the wood warps, it swells and it filters through the stone, seeping in through its pores, forming intermittent strings of drops that fall to the ground inside the abbey with the intensified sound of the emptiness.

My father decided to take Clara into our quarters the day the dean demanded even higher levels of performance from the workers. The herald informed us that henceforth we would work shifts of twelve hours by day and twelve hours by night and that those who wished to reduce their hours of rest in order to spend more time working on the "greatness of God" would be rewarded. The Greatness of God, now there is a paradox!

One of the men who decided to prolong his working day was my father. I remember how, following his instructions, we placed oil lamps all around the tower. During the night, the lights would let off a small swarm of sparks that rose in a never-ending line, indicating the way up. Sometimes, when there was a full moon, we could make out the silhouettes of the scaffolders hanging from their chains in the heights and the noise of their hammers, distant and precise.

It took eleven years to reach two thousand feet. Sometimes, Clara and I breathed in clouds. The fact is that they smell and taste the same as air. They have a slightly humid and thick feel about them, but no more. Without even realising it, we began to play a game of love up in those clouds. She would hide behind a cirrus so that I could only see her long, slender legs. Then her hand would appear, she would wave goodbye and she would turn and go up another step, succumbing to the fogginess and moving into the back room of the skies. I would run after her, making sure I kept my balance on the walkways, wavering against gravity. There is nothing behind a cloud, just an icy-cold dew which covers your clothes and slowly soaks through to your joints and mind and, before you know it, you feel lost, disoriented, stifled, incapable of getting your breath back. The wooden stairs lead some metres above and below you and everything is indescribably white: a perpetual, utter whiteness. Seeing Clara on the platform, dressed in red, appearing out of the paleness of the clouds is a spectacle of contrasts that is hard to resist. A kiss among the clouds, a caress on a plank of wood, an unhurried embrace and both our weights becoming part of the laws of physics. That was it. Yes.

Tiny, wee drops of rain falling upon the base of the cathedral. Thoreau never once came up to the platforms. He would always contemplate his creation from the same position in the cloister, collating the instructions he had given my father with the work being carried out. It was satisfying to see him become just another blot among the indifference of all the other insects, just one more amongst the crowds that would flock into Wescen every Sunday while my father's bell rang out far below.

* * *

Living under so much pressure is enough to exhaust anyone. Clara is now used to sleeping on the keystone of an arch and I, separated by a narrow embrace of an abyss, sleep on a column of ashlars. I can barely remember the last time I dreamt, and I now live in a slumber of unconsciousness. If I have survived, it is only because I am terrified of falling into a crumpled heap on the dome, brought down by vexation. In the midst of this insomnia, here on my column, any sound is amplified thousandfold. Thus, one night many years ago we clearly heard the abbey walls creaking under the weight of the tower, like two walnuts being crushed together vehemently. A few seconds later everything began to tremble and some stones came crashing down, exploding in the cloister and against the flying buttresses. One man invoked the Lord's mercy and someone gave him a mighty punch that sent him flying into the chasm. The noises and trembling went on until midnight and, as abruptly as it had all started, it all stopped. That night I could see a look of worry in my father's eyes and he was unable to sleep. He sat up looking over and over again at the plans of the old abbey, mumbling something about the tower being unable to hold out.

"Tomorrow I will have to talk to Adolphe Thoreau," I believe he said.

The following morning tiny drops of rain fell upon the base of the cathedral, reiterating the routine of the ascent. My father went down to talk to the dean. A block of stone which had come loose the night before had fallen through the shell of the dome and crushed part of the baldachin and the organ. Lying in the midst of all this destruction, the block of stone looked like a geometric challenge against the religious man's vanity. For the first time in ages I saw my father take charge and stand up for himself. He had spent the whole night by an oil lamp working out the weight the old arches would hold and he had reached the conclusion that one more block or an inopportune gust of wind might be enough to bring the whole tower tumbling down.

That was the last time I ever saw him. I do not know if he is still alive, if Thoreau lifted his sentence, if he was murdered or if he still goes to market on Mondays and looks nostalgically at the vertiginous lean, the impossible curvature of the tower that he began to build.

When my father disappeared, Clara helped me get over it. She made me believe that the world from up high, almost suspended, was a mood in its own right, a way of life that many mortals long for. When you have so little esteem for your life, any kiss or embrace, the little affection you get back seems even greater. It is as if everything were happening for the last time: the last kiss, the last caress or the last throes before calling it a day. Even the sky seems a different, brighter colour blue. You observe the deterioration of blues with deceitful delight and you feel the wind and the rain against your leathery skin differently. Any smell, no matter how imprecise, reminds us with nostalgia of what we might have been. Clara and Clara's body have come to fill the anguished void of my sentence.

I do not know how, possibly because I was the youngest worker or because I was the only one who still worked with any diligence at all, I became foreman of those men who dragged their empty stomachs in and out of the arches and walkways, pushing stones with their feet. Clara made sure they had enough to drink and set up traps to catch cormorants and eagles as I, plumb and tape in hand, measured the height and diameter of the tower. When we were lucky and a bird flew into one of the traps we would organise a party with raindrop stew, as Clara called it, freeing us from the dictatorship of porridge and compote the dean had us subject to. The nights we had raindrop stew, the light of the lamps flickering across the workers' bristly, hollow faces, everyone seemed happy. I would pull out some chalk and show them how little we had to go before we reached our aim. But the constant cracking noises coming from the walls never ceased to remind us that we were fighting not only in the face of adversity but in the company of sheer luck.

The workers kept dying. Many of them

had aged and despite their brawny constitutions, their muscles were cork-like, useless pieces of matter. More than once and more than twice I witnessed men falling into the void after their buckets of mortar. Not one of them so much as moaned on their way down, as they disappeared into the lower clouds plummeting towards the stained-glass windows of the abbey. We would cross ourselves, say a prayer and get on with what we were doing as if nothing had happened.

One day, as I was checking the verticality with the plumb, I realised that the tower was leaning slightly, just a couple of degrees. I remembered my father saying that mistakes, once they have been made at the base, multiply and safeguard each other, handing on the baton in height. Not a lot can be done in these cases. From that day onwards, I would go to sleep dreading that an untimely wind or a block of stone left lying around carelessly would reduce the tower to a huge heap of rubble.

I took great pains to calculate the remaining feet and the degrees of the deviation which undermined our chances every day. I gathered the men together and explained the situation to them. "By only placing every other block," I told them, "and building the next course alternately, the tower will be lighter. However," I warned them, "we are taking a great risk, a risk which under other circumstances would be inadmissible…" One of the elder men began to laugh. Under his mop of hair, I recognised him to be one of the carpenters from Angosta.

So we carried on, listening to the creaking in the walls and feeling the platforms shudder. The tower swayed like a reed in some kind of pendular ceremony brought about by the wind. Some of the blocks underneath us were slipping out of their slots and hanging over the abyss. At one point we were hearing the tower with every step we took, with every stone we lifted or plank we hammered in.

Under the circumstances, I doubt that anyone believed we would achieve our aim. Therefore, when I took out my plumb today and, after seeing it disappear into the clouds below, measured all three thousand feet, I was overcome a great feeling of happiness that I have been unable to express. When I told the five surviving workers, we celebrated in silence, looking at each other like castaways, as if a single word, a single gesture of happiness or annoyance could destabilize the unsustainable balance of the tower.

I could not get to sleep so I went to wake Clara up. I didn't shake her or make any brusque movements. I whispered softly in her ear and as she was just dozing on her arch, she asked me what was up. I asked her to come up with me and see our last sunset from the tower. She looked at me questioningly, as if accepting the last wish of a dying man. We walked up together slowly, listening to the echo of our shoes, the creaking coming from the planks of wood… We came up here and caressed the glass tip, which is scarcely bigger than a pin. I embraced Clara slowly on the platform which tilted. She began to weep and just then we saw, in the distance, through a tapestry of clouds, the Monday market and everything else. And it occurred to me that swallows are seldom mistaken in their predictions. It is going to rain. It is going to pour down tonight, with a gale-force northerly wind. But everything has taken on the same relativity as insignificant objects. "Clara, darling. Tomorrow without fail I will go down and speak to Thoreau."

Dionisio Martínez

Do Not Send Flowers to Your Mother

*D*ionisio Martínez was born in Cartagena in 1940. He has lived in Barcelona, Cambridge (Mass.), Brussels and Madrid. He has had several professions and has written ("and torn up," he confesses) many pages. He considers that "writing is like sharpening words as if they were old barbers' razors." He says that his story <u>Do Not Send Flowers to Your Mother</u> is not a tale but a segment of reality. A woman is carrying around a piece of paper torn out of a notebook in her handbag. There is a telephone number on it written in blue ink. It is a phone number that just might give her the chance to step into the forbidden world of feelings. But there are days when there just isn't time for anything.

Do Not Send Flowers to Your Mother

As she was reaching home, Monica made a mental note to ring her mother. Last night and the night before that she had got home too late to call her and it had been a long time since she'd heard from her. As she was walking across the garden, she saw that the shadow of a pine tree illuminated by the light in the living room was crossing the path and she imagined that Ernesto was probably still up.

She didn't want to ring the doorbell so as to avoid waking her daughter so she stopped at the front door to find her key. Her coat was draped over her shoulder, she had her laptop computer under her right arm, a red handbag in one hand and a heavy bag of shopping from the supermarket in the other. She leaned against the wall, clasped one of the straps of her bag between her teeth, balanced the bottom of the bag on her thigh which she raised, crossing her calf over the other knee and she thrust her hand inside it, trying to keep her shoulder up so that her coat would not slip to the ground. She rummaged around among her passport, her hairbrush, an oval-shaped silver powder compact, a few scrunched up bills and receipts, a Montblanc pen, some loose fifty and one hundred euro notes, credit cards, a Palm handheld, a scrap of lined paper which had been torn out of a spiral bound notebook with the telephone number of the man sitting next to her on her way back from London on a recent trip she had made there, her car keys, toothbrush, the remote control of the garage door, some recipes she had cut out of a magazine, the withered remains of a rose wrapped in cellophane, her mobile phone, a square of silver foil with four Caffenitrine tablets in it, lipstick, a small bottle of perfume, a plane ticket and two loose tampons, one of them in pieces. It took her a few minutes to find the key to the front door, but she finally took it out of her bag, unlocked the door, moved a scooter blocking the hall out of the way with her foot, threw her coat over the bureau, left the bag of shopping in the kitchen and went into the living room where Ernesto was lying on the couch, his shoes still on, browsing through a National Geographic. On the sole of one of his shoes there was a piece of green chewing gum, squashed and dusty with a hair stuck to it. The television set was still on. He hadn't taken off his jacket or his tie but he had managed to undo his belt. Only his bald head was visible over the top of the magazine. He didn't budge.

"I asked Ceferina to make a pie with the scorpion fish and leave it in the fridge. Did you find it?" asked Monica.

"I left more than half of it for you," replied Ernesto. "Elena had a yoghurt and four strawberries for dinner. She said that you know very well how much she hates fish pie."

Monica left her handbag on an armchair and, with her laptop still in her hand, she bent down and gave Ernesto a peck on the cheek, raising the magazine slightly.

"Your computer. You haven't brought work home with you, have you?" he asked. "At this time of night?"

"Tomorrow I'm going directly to the airport. I have to be in Barcelona at nine and I'll be needing it. Tomorrow we'll be closing the merger with the Catalans, at last."

Monica picked up the ashtray which was full of cigarette butts from the coffee table in front of the couch and walked back towards the kitchen.

"On Friday we're having dinner at the Salcedos'," called out Ernesto.

"The Salcedos'?" asked Monica.

"I've told them we're free."

"They're the most boring people I've ever met," shouted Monica from the kitchen.

"We'll have to leave early. On Saturday we have our paddle tennis class at half past eight in the morning."

She emptied the ashtray into the rubbish bin and, without going back into the living room, started walking up the stairs.

"Aren't you going to have any dinner?" Ernesto shouted out from the couch.

"I had a sandwich at the office," she replied from the landing, trying to keep her voice down.

She took off her shoes by scraping the heel over the edge of one of the steps and continued walking up with her shoes in one hand and her computer in the other. She stopped outside Elena's room. She got so far as resting her elbow on the doorknob, but decided to go straight to her bedroom. She left her laptop on the bedside table and went into the bathroom.

She washed her hair, then pulled it back with clips and plastic hairgrips. She cleaned her teeth and smeared a milky cream all over her face. She looked at her watch and realised it was too late to ring her mother. She put on her pyjamas and got into bed.

She was asleep by the time Ernesto came upstairs. He lifted her hand carefully and removed the book she was clutching to her chest. Soon after, he too was fast asleep.

At three o'clock in the morning, the telephone rang. It was on the bedside table next to Ernesto. He didn't move. The phone rang again. Just before it could ring a third time, Monica managed to pick up the receiver, having climbed over her husband's body and dug one of her knees into his stomach. It was her sister ringing to tell her that her mother had died.

She had never really recovered from the heart attack she had suffered scarcely a month before. Monica guessed what the news was as soon as she heard the phone ringing at that time of night.

Her sister said that she had received a call from their mother's night carer after the woman had telephoned for an ambulance and that she had gone straight to the hospital. What with all the agitation, she had left her mobile phone at home and hadn't been able to ring sooner.

"A doctor came and told me that there was nothing they could do."

"Did you see her?"

"Dead."

"I'll get over there now."

"They're going to take her to the funeral parlour on the M30. I arranged everything at the hospital. You won't be able to see her until eight anyway."

Monica hung up. She climbed back over Ernesto to her side of the bed and squeezed her pillow with all her might. She had barely seen her mother over the last years but now she felt disoriented, uprooted. The living pool in which the first steps of her life were reflected had dried up forever.

Some minutes later, she turned off the alarm clock and went downstairs very slowly to the kitchen. Through the window, she saw the wind shaking the trees. The ivy climbing up the north façade of the house was flapping against the bricks. She felt hollow. She was unable to get her head around what had just happened. She could only see the white, acidic light of the two rows of lamps that disappeared into some dark and confusing place. Her eyes were absorbing all of her strength. It was if she were escaping from herself out of them. All of her energy was flowing into her eyes while the rest of her body was coming apart. The white, ghostly, cold light on the trees. Just that light. As if her whole being had been reduced to a frozen gaze on the glass pane of a window, staring at those lamps and at the black dust, the smoke which the street seemed to be disappearing into.

She managed to make herself a cup of coffee and took it into the living room. She sat down on the couch, lifted her bare feet and stretched them out. She leaned her elbow on the back rest and let her head fall onto her hand. She felt cold and covered her feet with a cushion. She remembered her mother walking with her and her sister towards the school bus stop. Her mother was holding her sister's hand and she was walking behind. She was grasping her mother's skirt so tightly that her fingers hurt. The images were spinning around and around in her head like the blades of a broken fan, slowly, spasmodically. A fan that is about to conk out altogether. She went to have a sip of coffee but it was cold and bitter. She didn't drink it. She looked at the clock. It was already a quarter past five.

She went up to the bedroom and shook

Ernesto. When he half opened his eyes, she told him what had happened.

"How are you feeling?" he asked.

"A wreck, but I have to go to Barcelona. I have to be in Barcelona first thing in the morning. There's nothing I can do about it. I'm the only one with all the information. If we don't close this operation now, it will all go up in smoke."

"But Monica…"

"I'll be back as soon as possible. Maybe even this morning… Or first thing this afternoon. As soon as the agreement's settled I'll get on the first plane. Whichever way is quickest to get back."

"I don't think you should go."

"There's nothing I can do," she said, with an unsettled look in her eyes. She didn't seem to have enough air in her chest to be able to get her voice out, and her voice didn't want to leave her mouth. "You have to be at the funeral parlour at eight o'clock, Ernesto. Take Elena with you."

"Elena?"

"She turned thirteen in December, remember."

"Twelve," said Ernesto.

Ernesto was still in bed. Monica had a shower and brushed her hair slowly, taking great pains. Then she walked into her dressing room. She chose a grey suit. Not the red bag, she thought. She went back into the bedroom, picked up the computer off the bedside table and an empty black handbag which was on the chest of drawers.

"Flowers... Shall I send flowers?" asked Ernesto from his dreams.

"No. You'd better not. My mother had a real thing about flowers. She wouldn't let us order a wreath for my father when he died. My sister told me that she was quite annoyed that I sent her flowers at the hospital after her first heart attack.

Back in the living room, she poured the whole contents of her red bag into the black bag and then stuck her hand in to make sure her plane ticket was there. Her fingers rubbed the jagged edges of the piece of paper with the telephone number on it. It was ten days since she had got back from London. He had listened to her, watching her as if she had been in some distant place, his eyes dark and shiny like wet coal. She still hadn't returned the book of short stories he had lent her. She was going to ring him, soon, but she felt that first she should read at least a couple of the stories and she hadn't had time.

He seemed to be made of the special stuff. He was calm and relaxed. I have to get a grip and get off this course that is taking me nowhere. His thick grey moustache. His long, slender fingers that moved slowly as he handed her the book. The small blue veins on the back of his hands. On that particular flight she hadn't turned down any of the glasses of champagne the stewardess had offered her. She was floating. Wasn't it a bit too late in life…? She couldn't quite get her head around it.

When she had said goodbye to him, before getting into the company car that was waiting for her at the airport, she ignored the hand he stretched out to her and gave him two kisses, both of them on the same cheek, the second very close to his mouth, brushing his greyish moustache, pressing her lips against his skin.

"I'd like to return the book to you when I've finished it."

"There's no need."

She wanted to grab him.

"I'd like to."

Then he took out a pen, tore a piece of paper out of his spiral bound notebook, wrote down his phone number in blue ink and gave it to her. Cut. Change. She suspected that she had fallen in love, yes, in the space of two hours.

Monica got into her car in the garage. She placed her computer on the seat next to her and her bag, raincoat and umbrella on the back seat. The radio had forecast rain in Barcelona. She set off for the airport. She saw the day breaking as it began to get light. A purple stripe in the east that was becoming yellow as the sun got closer and closer to the horizon. The morning light began to reveal the sharp white lines on the tarmac, the distinct edges of the pavement, the cutting corners of buildings. (Her mother's body, with no profiles at all, lies in the darkness of the chamber, to the west.)

As she was heading towards the door of the airport car park after leaving her car, she decided not to go on. Turn around. Go and wait outside the funeral parlour until they open the door of the room they were going to place her mother's body in. She looked at her car. It was only fifty metres away but she had the parking ticket in her hand and she would have to pay before she could leave. As she was walking over to the automatic cashier, she ran into another one of the company managers.

"Where are you going?"

"Um, it's just that..." she hesitated.

"This way," he said.

So they made their way over to the airport departures building.

On the plane, she sat down next to the president with her laptop on her knee. The other two managers sat in the row behind them. She didn't mention her mother to any of them. During the first part of the trip she analysed a negotiation strategy. After breakfast, the president covered a yawn with his hand and closed his eyes. Monica took her powder compact out of her handbag, snapped it opened and looked at herself in the little mirror under the lid. She was biting her lower lip and at the same time, sticking out her top one. She could see her top front teeth and canines. One second. It was exactly the same face, like a rabbity smile, that her mother used to pull a lot. She touched up her lipstick and brushed her hair again.

The plane landed. All four of them turned their mobile phones on at the same time and set off towards the doors of the airport. It was raining. The head of public relations of the company they were negotiating with was waiting for them outside in his car. Only three would be able to fit and they all offered their seats to Monica. She claimed that she had to make some urgent phone calls and, believing that they must have been confidential, none of the men insisted.

She took a taxi. She put the computer vertically next to her on the seat and clutched it to her hip. She opened her bag to get out a tissue but couldn't find one. She pricked herself on a thorn, then took the withered rose out of her bag, opened the window and threw it out.

First of all she rang the office. She told her secretary about her mother. Her secretary asked her if there was anything she could do.

"Cancel all the meetings I have tomorrow

morning. I don't know… I might have time to… God knows what time they're going to have the funeral."

"What a bad time to die, poor thing," said the secretary.

Then she rang the house and spoke to Ceferina. She told her the news and Ceferina, who had spent the odd Sunday taking care of her mother, burst into tears.

"Ceferina, today only my husband and daughter will be home for lunch. Please try not to make one of your scenes. And make them some…," she pulled out the recipe cuttings from her bag. (A wooden rectangle with her mother's body on it is placed in the huge illuminated fish tank.) Once again, her hand brushed the jagged edge of the scrap of paper with the telephone number on it inside her bag. "I can't think…" She ran her eyes over one of the recipes. "Just make them anything. Or you could take out the fish pie that was left over from yesterday. Whatever."

She looked at her watch: the funeral parlour would be open by now. The taxi went around the Plaza de España. The two tall red brick bell towers at the bottom of the avenue that lead to the fair pavilions seemed to float in the grey air. Suddenly she was overcome by a feeling of transgression, of guiltiness. Her hands were dirty, she had a pain in her ribs and a metallic taste in her mouth.

She rang Ernesto and her sister but their mobile phones were switched off. She took her Palm out of her bag and looked for her aunt's phone number, her mother's sister. She wasn't at home either. She must have heard the news and gone to the funeral parlour. She tried her two cousins but they weren't answering either. (She has been called to the parched embrace of the earth at a time that only Monica ignores.) She imagined all of them, without her, before the corpse.

Another set of traffic lights. She might be

late for the meeting. A car in front of the taxi had stopped at the lights when they had not yet turned red and it was taking its time setting off when they eventually turned green again. She looked at herself in the rear-view mirror and smoothed her hair down with both hands.

Clinging to her mother's skirt. Two blond plaits, nervous, bulging blue eyes, her eyelashes constantly fluttering and her navy blue school uniform. The physical contact with her mother, her body, without so much as touching it. The stiffness of her mother's skirt against her fingers. She rang her secretary again and asked her to give her the phone number of the flower shop in the funeral parlour or one nearby. She wanted to order the flowers herself. Quickly, because the taxi was nearly there.

"Monica, your mother didn't like flowers."

"What does that matter now?"

She rang the florist's. A bouquet was

better than a wreath. Eighty euros was fine. Of course! Take it there immediately. Yes, a black ribbon with gold letters. From your children Ernesto and Monica and your granddaughter Elena. No. I don't know if she still writes her name with an 'h'. She might still be using that stupid letter 'h' in her signature. From Monica, just Monica, that would be better. My credit card number? Just a second while I pay the taxi driver, please.

The taxi driver grumbled, gave her change of a hundred euros and a receipt.

"My commiserations," he said.

It was pouring with rain. She didn't want to go into the building in case they were waiting for her in the hall. She opened her umbrella and held her laptop in her left hand. Her raincoat was all rolled under her right arm. She put the bottom of the handle of her umbrella under her left armpit and held up the top part and ribs with her head. The rain was coming at her almost horizontally and the wind was gusty and strong. She clamped the telephone between her shoulder and ear and grabbed one of the straps of her handbag between her teeth. She raised her knee and balanced the bottom of her bag on it and looked for a credit card with her right hand. Again she rummaged through her Palm, her toothbrush, tampons, recipes, passport, the torn sheet of paper, pen, Caffenitrine and the bottle of perfume.

A metallic clicking in her ear.

"Don't tell me you don't accept American Express. Does it have to be Visa?"

She took three credit cards out of her bag. Wedged between them was the piece of paper with the phone number on it. She wasn't sure which card to use. The wind was pushing her. The umbrella was about to fly off. The rain was getting heavier. She read out the number on one of them and chucked all three cards back into her bag.

Again the metallic muttering.

"Do you really need the expiry date?"

She felt her feet were wet and looked down at the ground. She saw that the water flowing along the gutter was sweeping away the jagged piece of lined paper. It was heading slowly, in fits and starts, towards a sewer.

She goes after the scrap of paper while still looking for the credit card. She takes two steps towards it with her right hand still in her bag.

A man sticks his head around the door of the building and tells her that the meeting is about to begin. She can't be late. After all this, she can't be late. (Red flowers, yellow, purple next to her mother's corpse. Her sister looks through the window and stares at them.) She finds the card she is looking for. She reads out the numbers of the month and year which, separated by a slash, are engraved above her name. She keeps walking towards the piece of paper.

Her hair must look terrible. She can feel

it's damp and probably dishevelled from the wind. She stops. She clamps the straps of her handbag between her teeth and balances the bottom of it on her knee again. The rainwater is making the blue ink of the numbers run down the paper. She pulls out her brush and drags it across her hair. The piece of paper is very near the drain. In order to get it, she would have to stop brushing her hair, put her laptop on the ground and anyway, the number is probably illegible by now.

Patricia Suárez

Chicken Paprika

*P*atricia Suárez was born in the Rosario, Argentina, in 1969. She is a writer and playwright. She has published two collections of short stories, <u>Rata paseandera</u> (Rambling Rat) and <u>La liana</u> (The Liana). Her novel <u>Perdida en el momento</u> (Lost in the Moment) won the Clarín Prize and she has also written poems and children's stories: <u>Historia de Pollito Belleza</u> (The Story of Chicken Beauty), <u>Chiquito Ratón</u> (Moppet Mouse) and <u>Habla el lobo</u> (The Wolf Speaks). The story of <u>Pollito Pimentón</u> (Chicken Paprika) arose from her experience writing children's literature because she does not agree with the idea that children's writers should be underrated in the literary world or considered any differently to authors who only write for adults. "In both cases," she says, "literature is a playful and philosophical form of expression."

Chicken Paprika

Let me introduce myself. My name is Julia Hurtado. My father was French so my surname ought to be pronounced 'Hurtadó'. However, this is of no importance whatsoever; you may pronounce it however you wish. You may have heard of me because of the children's books I have written, <u>Marmots' Conference and Chicken Paprika</u>. Although I have written about twenty books, this last one was the most successful of all. It was translated into English, French and Serbian. The problem is that the Croatian students in Serbian schools refuse to read it. I don't know why. Some students bought the rights to make Chicken Paprika into a film. They were going to make the characters out of Plasticine and the sets out of paper maché. It's incredible to think of all the things that can be done with paper maché, a whole world. In the end they didn't get around to making the film because the company that was going to finance the project went bust. This kind of thing happens a lot in Argentina: companies and people tend to go bust before they even realise it.

I still have a contract with the publishing house to write a whole saga about Chicken Paprika: Chicken at school, Chicken on holidays, Chicken at the circus, Chicken at the zoo, Chicken, the magician's apprentice. The problem is that I can't conjure up a single word. I hum along to songs I listen to on the radio that are now fashionable. Sometimes I even write them down. Some of them are very beautiful. I sit down in front of the computer, I open a new document and all I do is change fonts. How would it look if I wrote in Century instead of Times New Roman? What about Garamond? Wouldn't it bring be better luck if I wrote in Book Antiqua? I spend my whole time doing that and by the end of it, I wish Chicken Paprika were dead. That someone would come along and gut him and eat him or make him into a stew. And that's not the right way to go about writing children's stories. The spirit is all wrong.

My best story is one about two clams who are in love. They live on a beach and are constantly being harassed by a hammerhead. But they fight him and overcome all the dangers thanks to the solidarity of the crabs and the prawns. My clams feel so happy about their victory that they kiss each other. Lots of people express their happiness with a kiss and that's a fact, not something I just made up. However, the director of the publishing house vetoed the story claiming that the amount of licking that went on between the clams was too erotic for him to be able to introduce the book to young children. Are we talking about clams kissing or what? That man is a pervert. If pornography exists in the eyes of he who watches it then that man is completely degenerate. Children's literature is full of such foolishness. One children's literature critic wrote that one of the recurrent themes in my books is the struggle for survival. He reckons I write Darwinian literature. He has no idea where I've come from or where I'm headed. He has no idea of the things that have happened to me in my life. If he had been born into the household I was born into and had to grow up with my parents, he would know what I'm talking about. Yet I did not defend myself when the review came out, I did not send a letter to the newspaper, in fact I did nothing. I simply mumbled to myself: "humiliate me, Lord, once again. You must be so used to it by now."

Even though I know how important it is

for an author to have her own room, as Virginia Woolf advised in one of her essays, I have only recently made myself a space where I can sit down and write. I used to write in another room but we moved the baby's cot into it. Then we bought a thick rug so that she could roll around and make noises with her rattles. Now I write upstairs in the attic. It's a tiny little room with a skylight that's barely more than a crack. I placed some pot plants just outside it with mallows and geraniums in them, and another with one single narcissus. For some reason, the winter killed them and only the narcissus survived. It's almost a metaphor, a very bad one at that, but the narcissus is beautiful. It sways in the August breeze, almost as if it were dancing. Sometimes these colourful little bugs come and climb all over it and eat away at its leaves. I believe they're called narcissus aphids. They keep me amused. They're pretty little things and they remind me of a verse of a poet that says, "Illness shines darkly, like a jewel." I try to distract them away from the narcissus by putting tiny pieces of cheese on the eaves but they never show any interest. I also put little bits of fruit in a spider's web. I know that it's completely ridiculous. I can't be certain whether by doing so, I am helping make the spider prefer melon or apple and thus forget about catching mosquitoes, or whether I am in fact offering it a more varied diet. I work up here in the mornings because it's when I feel more awake and attentive to the world of words, although I while away most of the hours doing what I already mentioned: reformatting the same blank document over and over again because my pleas do not reach the ears of the Lord and he won't send me even one measly idea, just a hint of something interesting for Chicken Paprika to do instead of sitting here in my head at a stalemate.

My husband is also a writer. He writes

novels and stories for adults and sometimes I think that this gives him a clearer sense of reality. He's not too sure about the difference between an elf and a goblin, for example. A few months ago he published his latest novel, <u>Baghdad Festival</u>, about a journalist covering the Iraq war. He got very good reviews in all the newspapers and it even looks like he may get a national or local award, if they ever get around to reactivating the national awards where authors were given a life pension. However, the novel of his I like the most is called <u>Ah! Maria, come</u>. It's the passionate love story of Maria, a poor young girl, and Rodolfo, a rich man who has bone cancer. My husband did a lot of research on the illness, and I suppose that in that sense, the novel is a bit depressing. You can find it on the bargain tables in the bookshops on Corrientes Street for three pesos. Any of you could go and buy a copy and tell me what you think. It's a great story. When I met him he was already a writer, a good one at that, and that was why it was imperative that we should live in a house where he could have his own study where he could write and lock himself away at night. He spends most of the night writing and listening to jazz. His window gives onto the courtyard and he often sits gazing at the climbing plant on the wall outside, he says. It's a beautiful creeper with fragile, trembling white flowers and it's a lot better than having to put up with old Gentile who climbs up to his terrace and spies on me with his binoculars to see what I get up to for so many hours in my attic or getting distracted by the Colman boy's shouts as he climbs the cypress tree with what seems like suicidal tendencies. My husband has always insisted upon his own space, his own study, and also a bedroom for his children, who were still very small when we decided to move in together. When he and his ex-wife got divorced they went through a very rough patch. They are lovely children, Natalí and Andrés, and whenever they come and stay with us they sleep in the room my husband and I made up especially for them. However, now that they are getting older we will have to fix up another room or maybe even move into a bigger house because it's not right for a boy and a girl to be sleeping together when they are adolescents. I admire the way my husband works. First he does a lot of research regarding the facts and then he invents a world around them. He jots down lots of notes in his little green notebook and talks to people who can give him a variety of views and information. He is only interested in the truth, he says, not approximations or adaptations of the truth. He likes the whole, unabridged, spherical, clear and obvious truth which stands out like a huge ball of Gouda cheese sitting in the dairy products section in the supermarket. I could never write like that. The closest thing I ever wrote to the truth was <u>The Story of Prince Kalandar</u>, a prince from <u>One Thousand and One Nights</u> who fell in love with a rubber duck. I remembered all the unrequited loves I have had in my life and I poured those feelings into Prince Kalandar, the desolation he suffers knowing that he is not loved by the rubber duck. Nobody reviewed that book and my publisher refused to answer my calls for six months, as if I had written the story to drive him to the wall, as if I were some kind of swindler. I really liked the story of Prince Kalandar. In a way, he reminded me of myself, at least physically. He was tall, bony, with skin so pale that it reflected the changes in the weather, the afternoon sun, the stars, the storm clouds. He was almost transparent. Now look at me, look closely. Can't you guess what's going through my mind? A few months after <u>The Story of Prince Kalandar</u> came out, a journalist came to interview me. He was a very young man and it immediately became very clear that at the college where he had studied arts, they had never taught him anything about children's literature. The only author he was familiar with was Hans Christian Andersen. He kept trying to connect the story of the ugly duckling with Prince Kalandar's rubber duck. He reckoned I had been influenced by the former. He had obviously completely misunderstood the phenomenon: the ugly duckling is essentially good whereas Kalandar's rubber duck is essentially bad. I explained it to him in these terms but he just looked at me with great pity. The photographer who came with him, on the other hand, had a much more precise idea about what the authors of children's books are all about. He took photos of me surrounded by my baby's toys, talking to a cloth puppet and finally he took me to a playground a few blocks from here and took a photo of me on the slide. The guy must have thought that anyone who spends their life writing children's book is a complete moron.

My husband's children are very similar to their mother whereas our daughter, Violeta, is just like me. My husband's ex-wife is a naturally blonde, serious woman. She walks slowly and dresses in dark, tight clothes made of chenille. She is so into herself that she reminds me of a pea in its pod. However, she is a tidy, exact, brilliant woman who will live to be one hundred. She has always treated me kindly and still rings to wish me a happy Mother's Day even now. I can't understand why my husband prefers me, a creature who lives in semidarkness, why he doesn't go running back to her and try and make a go of it. After all, she is the mother of his children. I don't ask him because men's decisions are mysterious, inscrutable. And yet I am like a night creature, a moth which manages to dodge time and time again the flame of the only tiny candle which burns in the darkness. Only for a short time was I a butterfly fluttering around in full light of day before I returned back to my semidarkness. The Lord plays games with me and humiliates me, as usual. I will also live until I'm a hundred. It will be my misfortune to take at least a hundred years to burn my wings, little by little.

My favourite children's story is <u>The Bat-Poet</u>, written in 1964 by Randall Jarrell, a very peculiar poet from Nashville, Tennessee. I read it for the first and only time when I was ten years old and I was studying English at an academy. It was a sepia-coloured book with delicate illustrations by Maurice Sendak. I have never read it again since then but I remember it well, and often. It's about a little coffee-coloured bat who decides not to sleep during the day, but keep his eyes open and watch everything that goes on around him. Then he tries to get the other bats to see the world the way he does, the beauty of the world. He writes poems that reflect his vision and becomes friends with a wise old owl and some cardinals. This is my favourite story because I also believe that writing stories is a way of showing others how you see the world. Sometimes it's delightful, other times it's a fiasco.

My favourite colour is violet. I couldn't say if it's the colour that suits me most but it is the most beautiful of the seven that make up the rainbow. Some four years ago I wrote a story called <u>Giant Love</u>. It was about a giant who lived very high up and the only way to get to his house was by climbing up a green bean plant. A very friendly, graceful little girl called Violeta would go up and visit him and they became close friends. It was a great friendship, the kind that lasts forever. When I became pregnant, I begged my husband to let me choose the name of our child if it was a girl. I wanted to call her Violeta. She was born on the 6th of January, just like a present from the Three Wise Men, and we called her Violeta. She weighed almost three kilos and when she opened her eyes they were somewhere between blue and black. She was incredibly beautiful. I would watch her and fantasize about what her childhood would be like, reading, having fun and criticising all the children's books I have ever written. Her birth was the most incredible experience the Lord has ever given me. We were so happy. So happy, back then.

I recently attended a conference on the importance of reading. In the auditorium there were three hundred school teachers all eager to be told tricks and advice about how to stimulate children to read books. I read my work with great difficulty, asking myself the whole time I was there what the hell I was doing there is the middle of that Sabbath of sad women. Why in God's name should one person have to give advice to another about how to stimulate reading?

Are there conferences on how to stimulate your appetite? I felt as if I was betraying my readers, children. I felt like shouting out, "Please forgive me! I promise I will never do it again. I will never give a talk to these insipid creatures, not even for money." I would never betray a child. I have never betrayed my daughter. Not even when the doctor recommended that new treatment at the expense of her suffering. I did not say, "It will be for her own good. Let them operate. Let them put her in the intensive care unit, let them fill her with tubes and take her away from me." I hate people who make others suffer in order to teach them something. "It's going to hurt now but it's for your own good." It's a sentence I loathe. Of course I regret my decision now and I see my ethics as sheer stupidity. I suppose one can learn to carry around one's own regret, to live with it, I don't know.

I'm not even able to write a story like the fable of the flute-playing donkey who learns to play by chance. My husband tells me I shouldn't push myself so much, that style should flow like water in a stream after the ice melts. There are people who live writing like an epiphany. One day they have nothing and perhaps in a couple of hours they have a marvellous story that just came to them in the form of inspiration because the Muses were bored and just happened to notice them. I have taken a lot of notes on stories I would like to write besides Chicken Paprika: there's Henry the Faithful, about a boy in the Middle Ages who sets off in search of a dragon's skin to cure the heartache of his king; Caty, the little sleepwalking girl, and many others. My head is bursting with ideas, with characters. The problem is that none of them seem attractive to me right now. I live with Chicken Paprika or with any of the creatures I invented as if they were living beings. Sometimes I could swear I see the shadow of a goblin next to the door, the luminous footprint of a fairy next to the bathtub. That's what it was like before. I would get up from my dreams and I would sit down and write and they would appear, flowing and alive. So much so that after it happened, some time after, my husband could see that I was lost and asked me, "Julia, tell me the truth. Do you believe in fairies and goblins and magic? Can you see them? Do you talk to them?" I didn't reply in order not to hurt his feelings and because I don't want to hurt anyone else ever again. I closed the shutters on the whole business of pain. But I would like to have replied that I only believe in platypuses, in echidnas. In the skill with which a mongoose will catch a cobra. In hares, when they stop paralysed before the headlights of the cars racing towards them.

The day before yesterday I read a poem that really moved me. In fact it was a Japanese song which is sung to the music of a samisen, a guitar-like instrument they play. I wrote it down because I thought it might help me to write something about birds or about death. But I was unable to produce a single word. I just sat there biting my lips. It went like this:

Look at the trees:
three cedars and three pear trees,
there are six in all.
On the bottom branches,
the ravens' nests.
On the top branches,
the sparrows' nests.
And what do the pigeons coo?
One hundred steps to the cemetery
And a hundred more and another hundred.

The nights are long now and when my husband is not shut away in his study we spend them lying together in our bed that, despite being a standard size now seems as spacious as an imperial-sized bed. I put my hand in his, warm and robust, and he closes it around mine as if it were a frightened little bird. I ask him to tell me about our daughter's birth: the moment my waters broke, the first contractions, the taxi, the delivery room. He asks me if I dream of Violeta and I tell him that I don't, that when I sleep I only gaze at ivy. He says that he does dream about her and that he believes that God gave us the faculty of dreaming so that the dead can communicate with us or so that we can meet up with those who left us behind. "What's she doing there?" I ask, but he is unable to answer because he breaks down and begins sobbing. He cries with a comical whistle and it's pathetic when this happens. It confirms something I once heard in a film where one toy says to another that the meaning of his existence is to be loved by a child.

I would like to write about pain some time but my publishers don't want Chicken Paprika to suffer. They think that children should not know what it is to suffer, at least not through children's books. I tell them that what is not human is to bypass the sphere of pain. A person who does not suffer in life misses out on a portion of things. They claim that pain ought to be discreet; I say that this concept is false and mean. People who say that are pathologically selfish. I feel like the coachman in that story where he wants to tell his sorrows to some of the passengers but nobody will listen to him. He moans and groans. "Who will listen to my sorrows?" I am a saucepan without a lid. I am a winter mosquito. Pain can crucify you, can make you feel that you are completely insane just because you talk over and over again about something which others don't want to hear. Maybe they are right because there is something intrinsic to pain which makes it impossible to transmit. Yes, that's it. When I sit down in front of the computer in my own room and I look at my single narcissus, the survivor, swaying every morning in the breeze, I ask, sometimes out loud and sometimes in a whisper, "who cares what noise the wind makes, dejected, going around in circles during the small hours when none of the bars are open?"

One day we will turn the cot into firewood for our new heater, one day, the image I have of her in my head will begin to vanish and maybe this, the act of forgetting, will bring me some kind of relief. You can never tell. They say that when a wound is not painful, the scar hurts. It's quite likely. My chair is not very soft and I am always uncomfortable here, possibly because I am always perched on the edge of the chair. My fingers rapidly type out a text on the blank document. It is Chicken Paprika begging, "do not humiliate me any more, Lord. Lift me up in my hour of tribulation. That is your job, it's what a good Lord should do. Do not abandon me here amidst the ashes. My heart beats loud and fast. Press it against you own which is where it will shatter in the end." Then I paint the whole text and I change the fonts: Arial, Times New Roman, Bookman Old Style. Then I delete the whole lot: you cannot write stories for children with a spirit in this kind of state. You just can't.

Eloy Serrano Barroso

Nativity Scenes

Eloy Serrano Barroso *was born in Madrid in 1953. He has always been a writer, but in an impulsive, emotional kind of way. When in the year 2000 the newspaper 'El Mundo' began a collective novel on internet called <u>La rebelión de los delfines</u> (Dolphins rebellion), published by Espasa en 2001, he participated in three chapters of the literary experiment. Since then he has written many short stories, some of which have been published on the internet and others in printed collections.*

He works as a psychologist and understands literature as a way of playing with life, a way of removing what is useless and tedious. "You only have to find the right look and the way of expressing that look which can save us from the daily grind."

Nativity Scenes

Mummy woke me up early and asked me to help her set up the nativity scene. When I got out of bed the children of San Ildefonso had already began singing out the winning lottery numbers on the radio. After having my biscuits and milk I went into mummy and daddy's room. Mummy climbed the ladder we keep in the junk room and started handing me the boxes on the top shelf of the wardrobe. I piled them up on the bed. They were cardboard boxes. Some of them were shoe boxes; others were cake and biscuit boxes, and there were some I couldn't work out but they all had daddy's handwriting on them: shepherds and farm animals;

washerwomen and ducks; well and mill; Three Wise Men... When she passed me the box with Herod written on it, my hair stood on end and I got goose pimples because the priest who has been teaching us religion this year at school has put the fear into us. He has been telling us in a really scary voice that Herod used to cut the heads off newborn babies. "Only baby boys," he says, slicing his hand across his throat as if he had a knife in it. Then I imagine Herod with the head of a baby in his hand, dripping with blood and the baby's eyes look like those of a madman and they don't stop staring at me.

"Snap to it, will you?" shouts mummy from up the ladder. "If you don't hurry up your brother will wake up before it's finished and he'll start moving everything around."

I left the box with Herod and the others on the bed. Mummy kept passing me more boxes but she didn't stop grumbling or shaking her head.

"Why isn't daddy helping us?" I asked.

"It seems that your father has better things to do," she replied without looking at me. "And believe me, the only reason I'm doing the nativity scene is because of you. Otherwise…"

After getting all the boxes out, we took them into the living room. Mummy had placed a big board in a corner on top of two big boxes of detergent. She got a pencil and started drawing lines on the wood. "This will help guide us," she said. Suddenly we heard the front door open and then shut. Mummy stopped drawing and sat there with her mouth open. Then daddy poked his head around the living room door which was ajar.

"I'm back," he said, and vanished again. Mummy's lips tightened and she kept on drawing the same lines over and over again. She was pressing so hard that she ended up breaking off the point of the pencil. After complaining for a bit, she took the moss out of some bags and asked me to help her spread it out over the board, taking care to keep to the places she wanted me to put it. Then we did the same with the sawdust and we put down pieces of silver foil to make the river, which crossed the board from one side to the other. Mummy didn't stop sighing and bashing everything with the palms of her hands: the moss, the sawdust, the silver foil... the same as when we used to make sand cakes on the beach. From time to time she'd look towards the living room door with her lips pursed, as if wanting to see if daddy still had his head around the door.

I thought to myself that I preferred the nativity scenes we had set up other years because the grass was real and we had sand instead of sawdust and the water was also real and flowed like it does in rivers because my dad had got a little motor going.

I was thinking about all of this when my mother shouted at me again:

"What the hell's got into you today? Stop daydreaming, will you? You're acting very strangely."

I was about to say that she was the one acting strangely, she and daddy, both of them. I was going to ask her why they looked at each other so seriously when they bumped into each other at home, as if they were about to say something important and then didn't say anything at all. But I kept quiet; I just asked why we weren't putting water in the river this year, why the sand and grass weren't real.

"Ask your father... You should be grateful I'm doing this at all," she replied.

"What about the mountains?" I asked again.

"Shit!" said mummy. "I had forgotten all about them. Here, hand me that roll of paper." She was pointing at the sideboard.

Mummy removed the rubber band from the roll of paper and asked me to unroll it. Then, while I was holding one end of it and she was holding the other, she got some drawing pins and stuck the paper to the wall the nativity scene was resting against. That paper was sky, horizon, desert and mountains all in one.

"Didn't you want mountains? Well now you've got them," she said smiling as if she didn't mean it.

All of a sudden I felt like crying because mummy was acting all weird and I didn't know what to do to make her happy. And there I was, with a huge lump in my throat, when she smiled at me again.

"It's OK, darling, come on. It's not your fault…" she said, stroking my hair. She gave me a kiss on the cheek.

I didn't know what fault she was talking about but I was pleased to know that it wasn't mine. Though a bit later on, when she handed me the box with Herod and his soldiers in it, I thought she was lying and that something was my fault and that's why she was so sad.

"Help me put these figures here," she said.

I didn't want to pick Herod up with my hands but I didn't want to tell mummy I was afraid in case she thought I was chicken. Luckily, daddy came in just then. I said that I had to go to the toilet and I gave him the box. I spent a long time locked in the loo pulling faces in front of the mirror. When I went back into the living room, Herod was already in his castle on top of the cork pieces that looked like rocks and the soldiers were at his side: one on his left and one on his right. Daddy had gone and mummy's eyes were really red, as if she had been crying.

When the nativity scene was finished, mummy went and woke Juanito up. She picked him up and showed it to him. He was pointing at everything while mummy told him what they were called: little baby Jesus, the little shepherds, the little donkey... It made me cross the hear her speaking like that, saying that everything was little, and also when she told him that he looked like baby Jesus. I was going to tell him the story about Herod that the priest tells us at school to see if it would make him cry but then I thought that he wouldn't understand it. He's only three and he's still a little runt. I didn't dare pick up the figure of Herod with my bare hands and squash it against him.

Luckily, my brother soon got tired of looking at the nativity scene and mummy took him off to have breakfast and after that he wanted to play with his paints and Plasticine. I really like the nativity scene because it's like having a country all of my own, although I preferred it when the grass was real and it grew almost as high as the figures and had to be cut. And when the water was real and not made out of silver foil. I don't know why this year it can't be the same as previous ones.

I spent all morning playing with the

nativity scene. I put my cowboys and Indians, my police car, my train, my ambulance and my fire engine in it and made up lots of stories. I got an angel with a silly face that was hanging from a tress and made him fly like Superman. He was more powerful than everyone except Herod. He didn't dare take Herod on. He wasn't even game to fly over his castle.

Then mummy called me for lunch. The three of us sat down and ate together, mummy, Juanito and I.

"Why isn't daddy having lunch with us?" I asked.

"Wait till you see the dessert I prepared for you today," said mummy, getting up and going to the fridge. She came back with a crème caramel and cream, put it on the table and left the kitchen.

I ate as quickly as I could so I could get back to the nativity scene. I let my brother play with one of my cars so he would leave me alone and then I pretended that the baby Jesus had been kidnapped. Some Indians came and took him away from the stable and hid him in the mill. They left a note saying that they would only let him go when they were given the Christmas star in return. The Indians were tired of having to light fires all night in order to be able to see each other and they wanted the star so that they could hang it over their camp and have lots of light. Mummy says that Juanito looks like baby Jesus but I don't think so.

I had to stop playing because aunty Micaela came over to see us. She looks a lot like mummy, or more like mummy dressed up as an old woman. She gave us a bag of sweets, for Juanito and me. "They're for you to share like good brothers," she said. She also said that we had grown really tall and that Juanito looked like a cherub. Then mummy told us to go and have our afternoon tea and watch the cartoons on television because she and aunty Micaela had things to talk about.

It was a long time before she called us again and asked us to say goodbye. Mummy and Micaela both had red eyes. "You have to be very good to mummy," my aunty said and she squeezed me so hard that it hurt. I was about to tell her that I was already good to mummy but I couldn't get my voice out. Then she gave my brother a hug but she didn't say anything to him.

I went back to play with the nativity scene. The baby Jesus was still kidnapped. The angel with the silly face was going to save him but he kept getting waylaid by other adventures: stopping the train from derailing, making sure a little boy didn't drown in the river... Then daddy came home and gave me the shock of my life when he put his hand on my shoulder.

"Come and have dinner. You're a million miles away," he said. That's what he always says when he comes into my room and sees that I have a book in my hands but I'm looking out of the window.

"Daddy, why isn't anything real this year? Why are the mountains and the river and the grass all fake?"

Daddy stroked my hair, put his hand in his pocket and pulled out a little figure.

"Look what I got for you so you can put it in you nativity scene," he said.

It was a man squatting down having a poo.

I laughed but I bet he would have told me I was disgusting if I had bought it.

"Daddy, why don't we leave the nativity scene out forever? Then we could play with it every day," I said.

Daddy then started going on about traditions. I couldn't really work out what he was talking about but I did understand that it would get put back in the wardrobe as soon as Christmas was over.

"As if you cared about traditions," said mummy abruptly from behind us.

I didn't know what mummy meant either, but they had been saying things to each other that I couldn't understand for some days. They were talking really weirdly, as if they had a secret that they couldn't share. While we were having dinner, some chicken that mummy had made, they kept on at it.

"You could ask your father to take you to see the toys now that he's on holiday," said mummy.

"Perhaps mummy could take you, because I'm going to be tied up," said daddy.

And they spent the whole dinner talking like that while I sat in silence because I thought it was silly to repeat what everyone could hear perfectly well. And because I didn't know what to say, I asked if we had won the lottery.

"Yes, darling. I really hit the jackpot this year," said mummy staring at daddy. Her lips tightened again. Daddy bent his head forward over his plate and began sucking his chicken bones.

That night, after I had gone to bed and I

was half asleep, I was woken by their voices on the other side of the wall.

"Go, just go if that's what you want. I won't be wasting any tears over you," said mummy, and then she started crying like a puppy behind a closed door.

"Don't cry," said daddy, over and over again. "Don't cry." I hid my head under the pillow but the voices weren't going away and they reminded me of rats scratching at the wall.

I don't know why but I suddenly thought of Herod. He had his bloody knife in his hand and he was coming down the mountain attacking all the other figures in my nativity scene. Then he turned his head and looked at me. "I know where you are and I'm coming to get you," he said. He had a horrible smile. Then he made his way along the corridor and reached my bedroom door and stood there, on the other side of the door. I could hear him breathing so loudly that it drowned out mummy and daddy's voices.

Yesterday I got out of bed really late. Mummy didn't come to wake me up. When I went to the nativity scene, I found Herod on the floor with a broken arm and head. It must have been my brother, who can't keep his hands off my things. I thought that I would get into trouble, as usual. But when I told mummy she just said, "it doesn't matter. I'll put him back together for you. If only everything were so easy to fix." She said it in a very loud voice, as if I were at the other end of the house and not standing next to her. Then she picked Herod up off the floor and carried all the pieces of him in her hand, as if he were a little bird. After a while she came back and said, "There you are. Don't touch it until it's dry." Then she put Herod back at the top of the castle.

When I looked at Herod I was no longer afraid of him. His head was twisted and his arm looked as if it was on the wrong way around. He reminded me of the tramp who begs at the door of the church on Sunday. I was brave enough to pick him up and walk him all around the nativity scene. All the other figures laughed at him and kicked him out. The hens and pigs went and took over his castle. Finally, some shepherds threw Herod into the river and it was a pity that there wasn't real water in there.

I was happy because mummy hadn't told me off and because I wasn't frightened of Herod any more. But then daddy didn't come home for lunch or dinner with us. Mummy looked all serious and started moving around the way I do when I've just got up and I have to go to school and I don't really know what I'm doing. Later on, when I was already in bed, daddy came home and they started shouting again.

"Be quiet. You'll wake the boys up," said daddy.

"I don't care. Maybe it's about time they knew what kind of father they have."

But I didn't want to know. I just wanted them to shut up. But they wouldn't shut up.

Then I thought about Herod again, but Herod was wounded and everyone was laughing at him. When he looked at me he said the same thing he'd said the night before: "I know where you are and I'm coming to get you." But this time I felt sorry for him. I began to cry and hid my head under the pillow and covered my ears so as not to hear the shouting, but the shouting didn't stop.

Today when I woke up I didn't feel like playing with the nativity scene. It's all rubbish, the fake grass, the river made out of tin foil, the mountains... A star with a tail on it is stupid and the baby Jesus deserves to be kidnapped. I heard my mother shouting from the kitchen. "You'd better not come back, you bastard!" Then I heard the front door slam. Mummy shouts a lot and sometimes she says "shit", but she never swears. Only today. Then I felt like getting a hammer and smashing the nativity scene to smithereens. I didn't do it because of mummy, because I want her to stop acting so weirdly. However, I did step on the man doing a poo. I put him on the floor and I stamped on him as hard as I could until all that was left of him was a pile of sand. Then I got the angel with the silly face and I painted him with my watercolours. I painted his wings black and his hands and eyes red, as if they were covered in blood. While I was painting him I wasn't afraid but when I hung him off Herod's castle and he glared at me, I felt really frightened again.